For Davy, Marcus & Michael

minedition
North American edition published 2014 by Michael Neugebauer Publishing Ltd. Hong Kong

Edited by Brigitte Sidjanski
Text and illustrations copyright © 2010 by Marcus Pfister
Original title: Der kleine Mondrabe
English text adaption by Kathryn Bishop
Rights arranged with "minedition" Rights and Licensing AG, Zurich, Switzerland.

Michael Neugebauer Publishing Ltd., Unit 23, 7F, Kowloon Bay Industrial Centre,
15 Wang Hoi Road, Kowloon Bay, Hong Kong. e-mail: info@minedition.com
This book was printed in April 2014 at L.Rex Printing Co Ltd.,
3/F., Blue Box Factory Building, 25 Hing Wo Street, Tin Wan, Aberdeen, Hong Kong, China
Typesetting in Cafeteria, printed on FSC® certified paper.
Library of Congress Cataloging-in-Publication Data available upon request.

ISBN 978-988-8240-81-4

10 9 8 7 6 5 4 3 2 1
First impression

For more information please visit our website: www.minedition.com
Please visit also Marcus Pfister's website: www.marcuspfister.ch

Marcus Pfister

# THE
## LITTLE
# MOON
# RAVEN

Translated by Kathryn Bishop

minedition

Three old ravens perched on their branch, completely and utterly bored.

"Nothing happens here," croaked the first.

"Nothing has ever happened here," groaned the second.

"Not true, not true," protested the third. "Have you forgotten
the little raven with the silver wings?"

"Silver wings! He only had silver wings in your dream."

"You've forgotten!"

And so the old raven began to tell the story.

All the new little ravens in our flock had hatched,
except one.
But soon this last egg started to crack,
and in no time at all a tiny little something
poked its hungry little beak out.

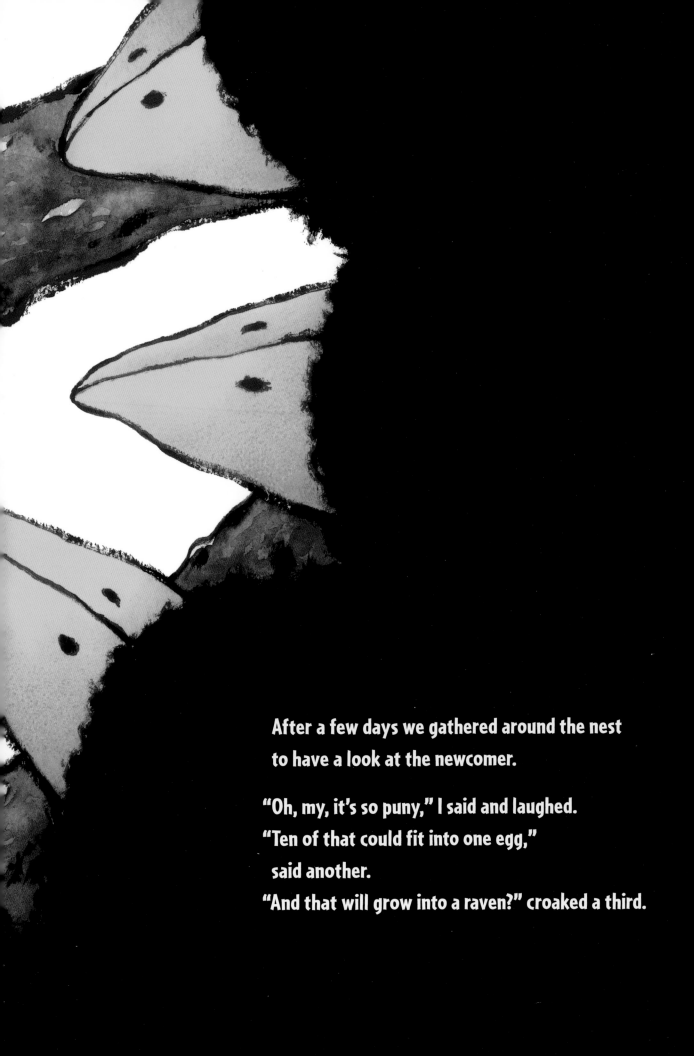

After a few days we gathered around the nest
to have a look at the newcomer.

"Oh, my, it's so puny," I said and laughed.
"Ten of that could fit into one egg,"
 said another.
"And that will grow into a raven?" croaked a third.

The little raven really was incredibly small.
Maybe that's why we started picking on him and bullying him
whenever we could.
He wanted to play with us, but we never wanted him.
"Why, you hardly have feathers, and you can't even fly yet!"
I told him once.
We were really mean to him.

The little raven's black feathers
began to grow and get thicker.
He was ready for his first flying
exercises.

He started with a clumsy flutter of his wings.
This was followed by his first hop from a branch and then his flights
got longer and longer.

He was gifted and agile,
and soon became the best flyer
in our flock.

"Can I play with you now?" the little raven asked us one day.

"Of course," I said. "You just have to fly up to the moon,
 and when you come back we will play with you."

"To the moon?" asked the little raven nervously.

"There's nothing to it," I said.

"We used to do it every day, when we were your age,"
 said the other crows, cawing happily.

That evening I watched the little raven staring up at the bright silvery moon.

Suddenly he took off.

He flew higher and higher.

I should have stopped him.

I should have told him it was a bad joke.

But I said nothing.

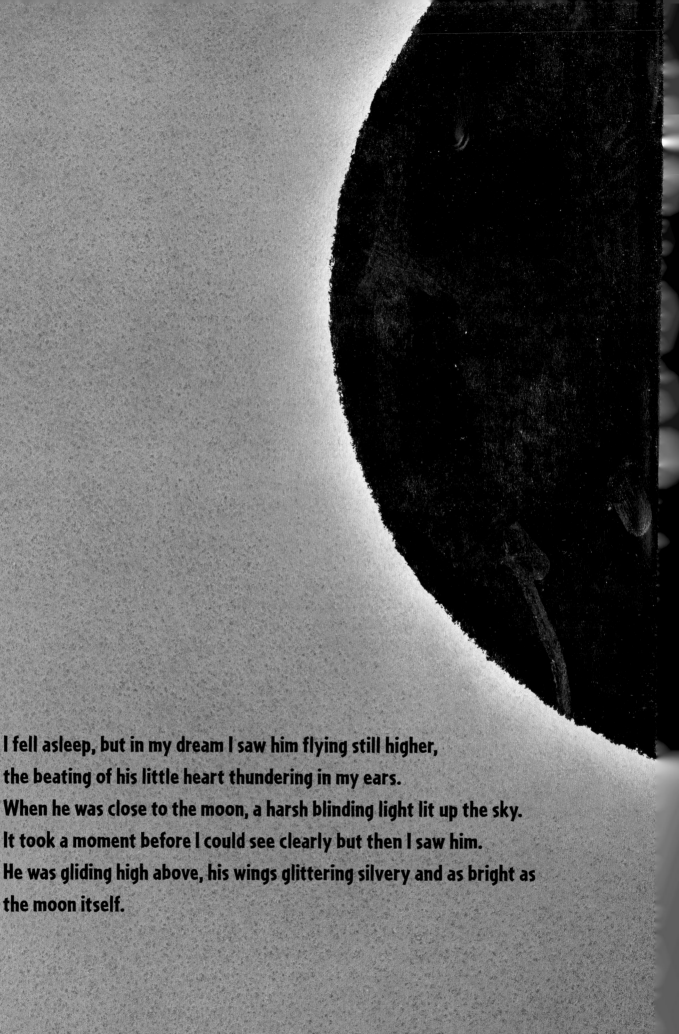

I fell asleep, but in my dream I saw him flying still higher,
the beating of his little heart thundering in my ears.
When he was close to the moon, a harsh blinding light lit up the sky.
It took a moment before I could see clearly but then I saw him.
He was gliding high above, his wings glittering silvery and as bright as
the moon itself.

Then he began to lose power. The beautiful silver wings were probably
too heavy. They seemed to pull him down. And he rolled and spun towards
the earth.
I opened my beak to scream but then his heavy silver wings caught the
wind above me.

I woke up completely confused and could not sleep a wink for the rest
of the night.

The next morning we found the little raven.
He was lying in a hedge close to our oak tree.
I was sure he had come closer to the moon
than any other bird.
The little one had the heart of a real fighter, but now
he lay there lifeless.
We all leaned over him and waited for some sign of life.

His mother sobbed quietly, and I was afraid.

Then the little raven suddenly opened his eyes.
His mom hugged him, and the little one said very softly,
"I didn't make it."
No one, except me, understood what he meant;
and I knew exactly.

"We didn't make it either," I stammered.
"I told you that just to get rid of you.
I never thought that you would really try to
fly to the moon. Can you ever forgive me?"

Instead of answering, the little raven rose into the air
and called, "Come on, let's play!"

It was only then that we noticed the silver feather
shining in the little raven's wing.
Together we followed him up into the bright,
clear morning sky.

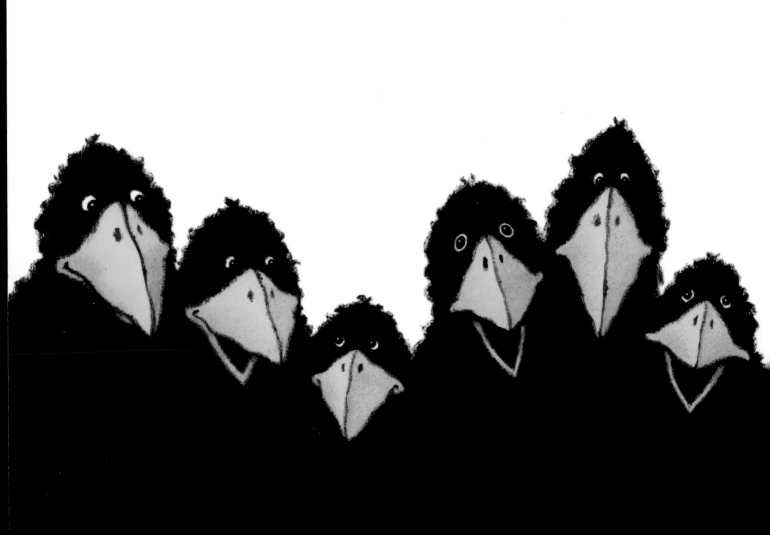